The Secret Warning

by Susan Blackaby
illustrated by Len Epstein

PICTURE WINDOW BOOKS
Minneapolis, Minnesota

Editor: Shelly Lyons
Designer: Abbey Fitzgerald
Page Production: Michelle Biedscheid
Art Director: Nathan Gassman
Associate Managing Editor: Christianne Jones
The illustrations in this book were created digitally.

Content Adviser: Brian S. Hook,
Associate Professor, Department of Classics
University of North Carolina Asheville

Picture Window Books
5115 Excelsior Boulevard
Suite 232
Minneapolis, MN 55416
877-845-8392
www.picturewindowbooks.com

Library of Congress Cataloging-in-Publication Data
Blackaby, Susan.
The secret warning / by Susan Blackaby ; illustrated
by Len Epstein.
p. cm. — (Read-it! chapter books. Historical tales)
ISBN 978-1-4048-4064-5 (library binding)
[1. Vesuvius (Italy)—Eruption, 79—Juvenile fiction. 2. Vesuvius
(Italy)—Eruption, 79—Fiction.] I. Epstein, Len, ill. II. Title.
PZ7.B5318Se 2008
[Fic]—dc22   2007032889

Table of Contents

Words to Know

harbor—a sheltered place along a coast where ships and boats anchor

Misenum—the place in southern Italy now known as Cape Miseno; an ancient Roman port

Roman Empire—ancient Rome's political territory; it was at its strongest point about 2,000 years ago

stylus—a writing tool used with a wax tablet in ancient Roman times

volcano—an opening in the ground from which hot rocks, gases, and steam pour out

Roman Numerals

Roman Numeral	Number
I	1
II	2
III	3
IV	4
V	5

Roman Numeral	Number
VI	6
VII	7
VIII	8
IX	9
X	10

Prima was scrubbing the stone floor in the courtyard. Servant work was difficult, especially since Prima was now the only servant left in her master's household. Her master's son, Titus, splashed through the water.

"Titus!" Prima scolded. "Watch your step. I'm trying to work."

Titus sat down. He dipped his finger in the bucket and wrote his name on the floor.

Titus, his family, and their servant, Prima, lived in Misenum, a town in the Roman Empire.

The house sat on a hill looking over the harbor.
From the garden, they could see a volcano,
Mount Vesuvius.

Prima sat back on her heels. She pointed her
scrub brush at the wet letters.

"What does that say?" she asked.

"Titus," he said. He dipped his finger and wrote it again. "See? It's easy. Write your name."

"You know I don't know my letters," said Prima. "Write it for me."

Since Titus' mother's death a year ago, 14-year-old Prima had been left in charge of 7-year-old Titus and his baby sister. But Prima was also responsible for the household, and that was a big job.

Titus shrugged. Then he dipped his finger in the bucket and wrote Prima's name on the floor.

Prima had Titus write her name three more times. She watched closely as he made each letter. She wanted to remember exactly how he did it.

Prima watched as the letters faded in the sun.

"You're lucky, Titus," she said. "You get to go to school. You get to read stories and study history and science. Those are things I can only dream about."

"I'd rather look at boats," said Titus. "Can I go down to the harbor?"

"Yes," said Prima. "Be back in time for dinner."

That night in her room, Prima dipped her finger in lamp oil. Then she wrote her name on the windowsill.

Even though Prima was very busy, she always dreamed of attending school. In the Roman Empire, slaves were not allowed to attend school. Prima believed knowledge would bring her power and freedom.

"My name," she thought. "It's a good place to start."

The next day, Prima met Titus in the garden. He wanted to play games.

"Let's pretend I'm a powerful senator," said Titus. "You are my subject. You have to follow my commands."

Prima shook her head. "Let's pretend you're a teacher," she said. "I'll be your student. You are very strict. You make me study night and day."

Titus scratched his head. "What will I teach you?" he asked.

"You'll teach me to read and write," said Prima. "Do you think you can?"

"Of course," said Titus. "I could teach Skip, if he could sit still."

Skip wagged his tail.

"Can you keep it a secret?" asked Prima.

"Yes, I can," he said.

Titus picked up a stick. He cleared his throat. "Now, class," he said, "no talking. We'll begin with the alphabet. The first letter is *A*. It looks like this."

Titus traced an *A* in the dirt. He handed the stick to Prima.

"Your turn," he said.

Titus helped Prima learn the alphabet. Then he showed her how to put letters together to make words. The two of them worked together whenever they got a chance.

Prima was a quick learner. In no time at all, she knew the alphabet. Soon she could sound out words. She could read signs and posters in the market. Titus gave her a flat wooden tablet covered in wax and a sharp writing stick called a stylus. At night, she practiced writing on the wax tablet, which she kept hidden in her room.

Titus' father worked as an architect. Because of his job, he often traveled far from home. When he was gone, he left Prima in charge. When Titus' father was in town, he often worked at home. Prima had to be careful. Titus' father didn't know she knew how to read.

Prima thought Titus' father would be upset with her for learning to read while she was supposed to be working. Still, she took extra time cleaning up after dinner so she could sneak quick peeks at his scrolls of notes and plans.

III Reading Lessons

One warm summer day, Prima and Titus were in the garden. Prima had her mending heaped in a basket. Titus was about to start reading from a science text.

"I saw a note that was lying on your father's desk," said Prima.

"What did it say?" asked Titus.

"I don't know," said Prima. "The letters looked like scribbles."

"That's just a different way of writing," said Titus. "Writers copy things in script. It's much faster than printing. But it's harder to read. Lots of people can read print just fine, but they can't read script at all."

"Can you read script?" asked Prima.

"If I want to," said Titus.

"Teach me to read it, too," said Prima.

Titus rolled his eyes. "Teaching you is a big job," he said.

"It's nothing. Look at the job I do," said Prima. She pointed at the torn clothes she was mending.

Titus laughed. "OK," he said. "Now, listen to this. A smart man named Pliny wrote it. He knows all about nature and the world around us. This is what he says about earthquakes."

Titus started reading, "A terrible noise comes before the shock. Sometimes you can hear a murmur. It sounds like cattle, or angry voices, or the clash of an army."

Titus looked up. "Do you think that's true?" he asked Prima.

"It could be," said Prima. "People say that giants cause quakes. They say that giants like to visit the eastern slopes of Mount Vesuvius and stomp through the valleys. Each step shakes the ground. So maybe it sounds like an angry giant. I don't think it sounds like cows."

"Moo," joked Titus. "Here comes a really big rumble!"

Titus' father was gone throughout the entire summer. Prima had lots of work to do. Still, she and Titus found time to study. Prima learned to read script.

On a morning in August, Prima was sweeping the walkway. Titus ran past her, and she grabbed him by the collar.

"Not so fast," she said. "What did I tell you about staying clean?"

"I know," said Titus. He wiggled out of her grasp. "Father comes home today. I need to look neat and tidy."

"Where are you going?" asked Prima.

"I just want to walk down to the beach. Don't worry. I won't get a speck of dirt on my clean clothes," Titus said.

"See that you don't," said Prima. She went back to her chores.

Skip had paced and howled all morning. Now he was out in the garden, barking.

Prima did not want him to wake the baby. She checked to make sure the baby was asleep.

Suddenly, a jolt shook the house. It nearly knocked Prima off of her feet. Jars rattled in the kitchen. A cup rolled off of the table. A crack spread across part of the wall.

Prima usually did not worry about quakes. They rattled the houses in Misenum all of the time.

Still, this one seemed stronger than most.
It was followed by two more big jolts. Prima
thought of Pliny's words. She listened. Was there
any loud sound?

Skip was still barking. Then suddenly someone
pounded on the door.

Prima jumped. "I'm a bundle of nerves
today," she thought.

Prima went to the door and yanked on the
handle. The door opened wide. A messenger
stood before her. He pressed a scroll into her
open hand.

"See that your master gets this right away," the messenger said.

Prima started to explain. "He's not here. I don't expect him until late."

"See to it!" the messenger snapped. Then he hurried down the pathway.

"Who sent you?" Prima called. But the messenger was gone.

Skip's howling echoed through the courtyard. Prima grabbed the door frame as the house rocked again. She had a bad feeling.

Prima went into the house. Her heart banged in her chest, and her hands shook. She did not think twice. She unrolled the scroll and read the hasty writing. It was a message from Titus' uncle to his father.

My dearest brother—

Heed this warning! Deep cracks split the earth. The mountain slopes rumble and swell.

Disaster may soon strike. Take the children.

Go north now. Do not waste a second.

Prima was scared. But she knew the message was serious. The jolts that had rattled the house were proof that something was wrong. She realized that it would be up to her to do something now. And she had to act quickly.

First, she packed a satchel with food. She grabbed a coin-filled pouch and a small locked box from under the couch. The box held Titus' mother's jewels.

Prima went to her room. She got out her wax tablet and stylus. She quickly wrote a note to Titus' father.

Sir—

I have taken the children. We have fled to Cumae. You will find us at the temple square.

Your faithful servant,

Prima

Prima placed her message on the table next to the scroll.

Next, she ran to the garden to get Skip and tied a leash around his neck. She told him to wait by the door.

Prima then went to get the baby. The drowsy baby curled up in Prima's arms. She dropped her head onto Prima's shoulder.

Prima rushed through the house. She took one last look from the doorway. A packet of plans sat on the bench. Titus' father might need them. Prima stuffed the packet into the satchel. She pulled the door shut and tugged Skip to follow her as she hurried to the road. She had to find Titus right away. She had no time to lose.

Outside the house, the morning seemed like any other morning. Sleepy donkeys pulled carts. Neighbors gossiped. Children played.

A shopkeeper smiled and waved. "Hello!" he
called. "It's been shaky today! Where are you
rushing to with such a load?"

"A disaster may be headed this way," Prima replied. "I'm taking the children to Cumae. You should head north as well. Have you seen Titus?"

"A disaster? The quakes are common, Prima."

"Yes, but—" Prima said.

The shopkeeper was not interested in the news. He replied, "Titus came by a while ago. He was heading for the beach."

Prima waved and hurried on her way.

Prima went down the alley to the waterfront. She knew that Titus liked to watch the fishing boats, so she walked quickly toward the harbor.

Lots of people were at the shore. They were watching huge waves crash onto the beach. Prima pushed her way through the large crowd.

Suddenly Skip stopped and started barking. Prima pulled the leash, but Skip would not budge at all.

"Titus!" she thought. "Skip must know he's close by."

Prima went to the top of the stairs leading to the beach. She saw Titus near the water. Skip barked frantically.

Titus turned and saw them. He looked puzzled. But when he saw the fear on Prima's face, he came running.

"Prima," he cried. "What happened?"

"Nothing," she said. "Nothing yet, anyway."
Prima handed Titus the satchel. "We're going to
Cumae. I'll explain on the way."

Titus followed Prima. They walked through
the narrow streets until they came to the main
road, where they turned north.

Once they were on their way, Prima relaxed a
little. "Something is going to happen. I've had a
bad feeling all day," she told Titus.

Prima explained Skip's odd behavior to Titus. She also told him about the quakes that shook the house. And she told him about the message that had arrived for his father. "I know it was wrong to read it," she said. "But I had to."

Soon the baby was fussing. Titus was thirsty. The afternoon sun beat down on them. Skip would not sit still.

"Let's keep going," said Prima. "The sooner we reach Cumae, the better."

They had not gone very far when Titus
stopped to tie his sandal. As he kneeled in the
road, he turned to look back across the bay.

"Prima!" he said. "What's that?" Titus
pointed to the sky.

A tall plume of black and white smoke rose
out of the top of Mount Vesuvius. The cloud
filled the bright blue sky. At the same time, the
earth dipped and rocked.

Prima and the baby dropped down beside Titus. They watched the cloud billow down and cover the mountain's slopes. It seemed to boil and tumble as it moved.

Prima looked at Titus. She touched his white tunic. It was flecked with ash.

"We have to get out of here," she said.

Bits of rock and ash fell like rain. Smoke
blocked the sun. Prima held on to Titus' hand.
They stumbled along the road in the dark.

In the evening, they came to the outskirts
of Cumae.

"Now what?" Titus asked. He and the baby
were tired and hungry.

"We find the temple square and wait for your father," said Prima. "I told him where he would be able to find us."

Titus felt scared. "What if he doesn't come?" he asked.

Prima felt scared, too. "He'll come," she said. She hoped it was true.

Prima found a spot on the temple steps.

"Sit down," she said. "Have some food. We'll be safe here. We can spend the night here if we have to."

Prima reached out and squeezed Titus' arm. "You have been so brave, Titus. Your father will be proud of you."

Titus tried to smile. He stroked Skip's back. The dog pranced and huffed. He could not sit still.

Skip was making Prima nervous, but she tried not to show it.

Throughout the night, the ground shook. Red flares lit the horizon. Gold flames flickered in the sky. Titus and the baby slept. Skip and Prima watched over them.

The next morning, the sun glowed orange in the smoky sky. Prima knew they had to sit and wait for Titus' father.

Prima, Titus, and the baby passed the day on the temple steps. When it was time for dinner, Prima remembered the money. She was about to give Titus coins to buy them some food, when Skip started yipping and wagging his tail.

Through the haze, Titus spotted his father. He jumped up and ran across the square. Skip followed closely on his heels.

"Father! Father!" Titus called.

Titus' father set down his gear. He lifted his son up and twirled him around.

They made their way to the temple steps. Titus was talking a mile a minute.

Titus' father smiled at Titus as he set him down on the ground. Then, he bent down, picked up the baby, and held her in his arms.

"I arrived in Misenum last night," he said. "Everyone in the town was panicking. Flaming rocks poured from the mountaintop. Ashes fell in drifts. When I didn't find you at home, I was so worried. I thought that we had been robbed! Then I saw Prima's note. All of the roads were jammed with people trying to flee. I got here as quickly as I could."

He turned and stared hard at Prima.

"Prima," he said. "I didn't know you could read and write. What do you think I should do about it?"

Prima felt her cheeks get hot. She didn't know what to say.

Titus spoke up. "Don't punish Prima," he said. "I'm the one who taught her. You should punish me instead."

"No," said Prima. "Titus isn't to blame. I made him do it. I know it was a mistake. I'm very sorry."

"Well, I'm not sorry," said Titus' father. "I'm overjoyed, Prima!"

Titus and Prima stared in surprise.

"Your ability to read and write saved us," Titus' father said. "You have my thanks and my deepest gratitude. When we return home, I'll give you your freedom and send you to school."

Titus giggled. "That sounds like a punishment to me," he said.

But to Prima that sounded like a dream come true.

In the days of the Roman Empire, there lived a man named Pliny the Elder (A.D. 23–79). He was an observer of the natural world and wrote many works, but the one that survives is his *Historia Naturalis* (Natural History).

Pliny lived in Misenum, the setting for this story. Misenum is on the Bay of Naples. It is about 18 miles (30 kilometers) west of Mount Vesuvius.

On the afternoon of August 24, in the year A.D. 79, earthquakes rocked the area along the coast. However, people in those days did not realize that earthquakes and volcanic eruptions are connected.

Between two and three o'clock in the afternoon, Pliny's sister saw a plume of ashes. It rose for miles above Mount Vesuvius.

Pliny wanted to get a closer look. He started to sail across the bay. He did not get far before burning rocks and ashes rained down. Pliny realized that people in Herculaneum would need help. He tried to get there, but rocks and ashes choked the bay. He sailed to Stabiae. It was there that he was caught in a cloud of poisonous gas from the eruption.

Meanwhile, there was panic and chaos in Misenum.

Pliny's nephew, Pliny the Younger, and his mother ran for their lives. The eruption went on for about 20 hours.

When the eruption ended, Pompeii and Herculaneum were gone. They were covered in lava, mud, rock, and volcanic ashes. Hundreds of years went by before they were rediscovered. The letters written by Pliny the Younger are the only surviving eyewitness reports of what happened that day.

Today, Mount Vesuvius is sleeping. We do not know exactly when it will come to life again, but we do know how deadly it can be.

On the Web

FactHound offers a safe, fun way to find Web sites related to topics in this book. All of the sites on FactHound have been researched by our staff.

1. Visit *www.facthound.com*
2. Type in this special code: 1404840648
3. Click on the FETCH IT button.

Your trusty FactHound will fetch the best sites for you!

Look for more *Read-It!* Reader Chapter Books: Historical Tales: